A Novelization by Stephanie Calmenson
from the screenplay
Written by Caroline Thompson & Larry Wilson
Based on the Characters created by Charles Addams

SCHOLASTIC INC.
New York Toronto London Auckland Sydney

PARAMOUNT PICTURES PRESENTS A SCOTT RUDIN PRODUCTION ANJELICA HUSTON RAUL JULIA CHRISTOPHER LLOYD THE ADDAMS FAMILY MUSIC BY MARC SHAIMAN DIRECTOR OF PHOTOGRAPHY OWEN ROIZMAN, A.S.C. PRODUCTION DESIGNED BY RICHARD MacDONALD EDITOR DEDE ALLEN, A.C.E. COSTUME DESIGNER RUTH MYERS CO-PRODUCER JACK CUMMINS EXECUTIVE PRODUCER GRAHAM PLACE WRITTEN BY CAROLINE THOMPSON & LARRY WILSON BASED ON THE CHARACTERS CREATED BY CHARLES ADDAMS PRODUCED BY SCOTT RUDIN DIRECTED BY BARRY SONNENFELD A PARAMOUNT COMMUNICATIONS COMPANY

These credits are tentative and subject to change.

ISBN 0-590-45540-0

12 11 10 9 8 7 6 5 4 3   2 3 4 5 6/9

Printed in the U.S.A.   40

First Scholastic printing, December 1991

The Addams Family™

1.
Gloriously Gloomy

*B*ong. *Bong. Bong. Bong. Bong. Bong. Bong.*
The clock struck seven at the Addams family mansion. Outside it was a bright and sunny morning. Inside it was gloriously gloomy — just the way the Addamses liked it.

Gomez Addams was in the room of his long-lost brother, Fester. He was talking to Thing. Thing was the hand — yes, the hand — who lived at the Addamses' house.

"Just think of it, Thing," said Gomez. "Fester has been gone for twenty-five years now. For twenty-five years we've been trying to get in touch with him. Tonight we must try again."

It made Gomez sad to think of his brother. No one knew where on — or over, or under, or into — earth he had gone.

Thing took Gomez by the cuff of his pajamas

1

and led him to his wife, Morticia. Morticia always knew how to cheer up Gomez.

"*Cara mia!*" cried Gomez the moment he saw her.

Morticia was lying in her bed. Her chalk-white skin and jet-black hair were resting against her black satin pillow.

Gomez took Morticia's hand and kissed her from the tips of her fingers all the way up to her neck.

"Oh, you make me so unhappy," whispered Morticia, in her soft but husky voice.

"I try, my sweet," said Gomez adoringly.

Someone else in the Addams family was awake. It was Pugsley. He was nine.

"One more drop of bat blood and my potion will be ready!" said Pugsley.

The brew bubbled noisily. The smell was awful. *Gulp, gulp, gulp.* Pugsley swallowed every drop.

"Hee, hee, hee!" laughed Pugsley as he shrank to the size of a mouse. Well, a slightly tubby mouse. That was because Pugsley was a slightly tubby boy.

He slipped out of his boy-sized pajamas and ran to scare up some trouble.

He headed for his ten-year-old sister Wednesday's room. But Wednesday wasn't there. No, Wednesday, who looked just like her mother, with chalk-white skin and jet-black hair, was up in the attic having her tooth pulled. Granny was helping her.

"Weddy, Gwanmama," Wednesday mumbled. She was mumbling because one end of a string was tied to her tooth. The other end was tied to a trapdoor.

Granny, whose white hair stood out straight from her head in every direction, flung open the door. Wednesday's tooth popped out of her mouth and dangled from the string.

"Thank you, Grandmama," she said. She added the tooth to a box already half filled with teeth and glass eyes.

Just then, Lurch, the Addams family's seven-foot-tall butler, came to the door.

"Arrrrowwl!" he growled.

"Time for breakfast already? I'll be right there," said Wednesday.

Lurch couldn't find Pugsley. (He did not know that Pugsley-the-mouse was riding on his shoe.) He went to tell Gomez and Morticia that breakfast was ready.

"Arrrrowwl!" he growled.

"We'll be there in a minute," said Gomez. He was hitting golf balls out the balcony window. Thing, helpful as always, held the balls up one by one.

SWACK!

"I think I hit a good one!" cried Gomez.

A moment later they heard the smash and tinkle of glass. There was now one less window at the tidy house next door.

That was Judge Womack's house.

2.
Gate

The golf ball landed in Judge Womack's cereal bowl.

"Of all the neighbors in the world, I had to get the Addams family," said Judge Womack, shaking his fist in Gomez' direction.

Gomez, thinking the judge was waving to him, waved back happily.

"You can keep the ball, Judge!" called Gomez.

Beep, beep! The school bus came to pick up Wednesday and Pugsley, who was back to boy size.

When the mansion gate saw the bus, it opened wide. Gate had a mind of its own. It decided who to let in, who to keep out, and who to make miserable.

"There go our little dears," said Morticia, waving out the window.

A few hours later Gate had two more visitors — Tully Alford and his wife, Margaret. Tully was the Addams family lawyer.

Gate opened just enough to let in Margaret. But when Tully tried to get in, Gate slammed shut. Gate did not like Tully.

"Let go of me!" cried Tully. "I'm warning you!"

"Stop playing with that gate and come inside," complained Margaret. "The Addamses are your last paying clients, and we *need* their money."

The only way Tully could free himself was to rip his coat. So he did. Then he hurried to catch up to Margaret, who was already knocking at the Addamses' door. Soon they heard heavy footsteps and the slow creak of the door as it opened.

"Arrrrowwl," said Lurch, showing them inside.

Margaret was terrified of Lurch. She hurried to find Morticia. She wanted to talk to her about a charity auction.

Tully headed for Gomez' study. On the way, he saw a portrait of Fester Addams as a teenager. Even as a teenager he was completely bald. Fester was holding a candle. The candle was real. And strangely enough it was lit. Tully was studying the portrait when he heard Gomez call, "Greetings, old chap!"

Tully turned around just in time. Gomez flipped a razor-sharp sword in his direction. He held up another sword, and the two men began their usual fencing match. *Clink! Clink!*

While they fenced, Gomez signed the papers

Tully had brought him. One paper had writing so small, Gomez could hardly read it. He took out a magnifying glass.

"Hmm," said Gomez. "The Fester Addams Offshore Retirement Fund. What's this about?" *Clink! Clink!*

"Why, it's the perfect tribute to your dear, departed brother," said Tully. "I thought it might be best to put the funds in my name — for tax purposes of course."

"Of course," said Gomez, studying the paper. "Speaking of Fester, we'll be trying to reach him at our séance tonight. You and Margaret will come, won't you?"

"Um, well . . ." mumbled Tully.

"Great!" said Gomez. "We'll expect you at eight o'clock sharp. Make yourself comfortable, old man, while I get the money from the vault for our monthly expenses."

Gomez left the room and closed the door behind him. Tully followed quietly behind. He watched Gomez go into his den and pull a book from a shelf. It was too dark for Tully to read the title.

When the book came off the shelf, a secret panel opened, and Gomez disappeared inside. Behind the secret panel was the Addams family fortune.

"I've got to know the way to that vault," said Tully to himself.

He took a book from the shelf. But the secret

panel stayed closed. The book in his hand was called *Gone With the Wind*.

Maybe there's a secret code inside, thought Tully.

He opened the book. There was no secret code — only gales of wind that blew from the book and pinned him against the wall.

Meanwhile, up in the attic, Margaret watched as Morticia pulled out trunks filled with Addams family treasures.

"Ah, here is our rarest one," said Morticia. "It is a finger trap from the court of Emperor Wu."

"It must be worth a fortune. Are you sure you want to give it to us for the auction?" asked Margaret with a gleam in her eye.

"Anything for charity," said Morticia.

Margaret grabbed the trap and without thinking stuck her fingers inside.

Just then, Tully appeared.

"I think it's time to go now, dear," he said.

"Yes, I think you're right," Margaret answered quickly. She stuffed her hand with the trap into her pocket.

Margaret and Tully raced out of the house.

Gate was happy to see them go and it opened wide. But it slammed shut in time to catch Tully's trousers — just for the fun of it.

3.
The Plan

Tully dragged a heavy suitcase full of money into his office. He looked around for his secretary.

"Miss Bradbury? Miss Bradbury, where are you?" he called.

"Miss Bradbury is out to lunch," called an all-too-familiar voice from the other room.

"Oh, no, no, no!" whispered Tully to himself. "Not old Abigail Craven. She's the last person I want to see."

Abigail poked her head into the room.

"You're just the person I wanted to see, Abigail!" lied Tully. "I was going to call you this afternoon."

"Well, here I am," said Abigail. "And I've brought my son, Gordon, with me. You haven't met Gordon, have you, Mr. Alford?"

Tully took one look at Gordon and broke into a

9

sweat. Gordon was big. Gordon was strange. Gordon was scary!

"Is he the one you told me about, Mother? The one who owes you money?" said Gordon.

Gordon didn't wait for his mother's answer. He lifted Tully into the air and dangled him upside down by his ankles.

"Hold on! I can explain!" cried Tully.

"Mother, would you like him to explain upside down or right side up?" asked Gordon, jiggling Tully up and down as he spoke.

"Oh, Gordon. Have I told you lately that you are the apple of my eye?" said Abigail, watching Tully dangle.

"Yes, Mother. And you're a peach," said Gordon.

"I guess you can let him down now," said Abigail.

"Okay, Mother," said Gordon.

THUD! Tully fell to the floor headfirst.

"Now before you explain," said Abigail, "tell me, how is your wife? Is she still charming? Is she still spending lots of money? *My* money?"

"I . . . I don't have any money," whined Tully.

"But I lent you thousands of dollars, Tully. And now I want them back," said Abigail.

"I promise I'll give you the money soon," said Tully.

"I want to believe you," said Abigail. "And Gordon wants to believe you, too. Show Tully how much you want to believe him, my darling dumpling."

Gordon lifted Tully again. This time he swept him across the desk like a broom. Tully's briefcase flew down to the floor and popped open. Coins spilled everywhere!

"Look, Mother, money. He lied to us!" said Gordon, squeezing Tully's neck as he spoke.

"It's not what you think!" gasped Tully. "Those coins aren't mine. Gomez Addams gave them to me to pay off his monthly expenses. I swear it!"

"Did I hear you say 'Addams'?" asked Abigail.

"Yes, yes! They have a fortune. It's hidden away in their mansion. I tried to get it for you. Really I did!" said Tully.

"Ask him how hard he tried, sweetheart," said Abigail to Gordon.

"No! Sweetheart! Don't ask!" begged Tully. He was flat on his desk, staring up at Gordon's face.

Suddenly, Tully's eyes opened wide. It was partly because Gordon was squeezing his neck. But there was another reason. A bright bulb overhead was playing tricks with the light. It made Gordon look as bald as a Ping-Pong ball.

Tully had seen that bald head and face before. If only he could remember where. Where? Where?

11

The portrait! The portrait of Fester Addams! That was it! Gordon Craven looked just like Fester Addams.

Oh, happy days! Tully thought of a plan — right before he fainted.

4.
Good-bye, Gordon

Rain splashed! Thunder crashed! Lightning lit the sky!

In a tacky motel room Gordon sat facing his mother, Abigail. When Tully had regained consciousness, he had told them his plan. Gordon would show up at the Addamses' house that night, dressed as Uncle Fester. After he moved in, he could break into the vault. It was brilliant!

"I can't believe how much you — my little boy — look like this hideous creature," said Abigail in disgust, holding up the picture of Fester that Tully had lent them.

"You hurt my feelings, Mother," said Gordon, pouting.

"I'm so sorry. Did I say hideous? I meant handsome. Handsome creature," said Abigail.

"That's better, Mother," said Gordon.

"Just think, Gordon, we won't ever have to pull off another shady deal. We won't have to have anything to do with lowlifes like Margaret and Tully Alford. We won't have to make another penny for as long as we live. We'll be rich, rich, rich!"

"But, Mother, won't we get into trouble?" asked Gordon.

"Of course not. Tully's plan is perfect. For *us* that is. You move into the Addamses' house for a week. You break into the vault and steal everything. Then you disappear. We'll leave Tully behind to do the explaining," said Abigail.

"Mother, you are a genius!" cried Gordon.

"Thank you," said Abigail. "Now let's get started."

She covered Gordon's head with shaving cream, picked up a razor, and began to shave his head. Right before her eyes, Abigail's son was turning into the creature in the picture.

"Good-bye, Gordon. Hello, Fester!" said Abigail.

Meanwhile, at the Addamses' mansion, the family was getting ready for their big night.

"*Cara mia,*" whispered Gomez, with his arms wrapped around Morticia's waist. "It is a miserable night."

"I know, darling. It is perfect séance weather," replied Morticia.

Bong. Bong. Bong. Bong. Bong. Bong. Bong. Bong.

The clock struck eight. At that very moment, there was a knock at the front door.

"That must be Margaret and Tully. They're right on time," said Gomez.

"Arrrowwl," growled Lurch, opening the door.

Margaret froze with fear when she saw Lurch. No matter how often she came to the Addamses' house, she couldn't get used to the Addamses' monstrous butler.

Wednesday appeared right behind Lurch.

"Hey, small fry!" said Tully, reaching out to pat Wednesday's head.

Wednesday took three giant steps backward. Like Gate, Wednesday did not like Tully.

"Hello, sweetheart," said Margaret. "Would you mind undoing this?"

Margaret held out her trapped fingers, and Wednesday quickly set her free.

"Now we can get out of here!" whispered Margaret.

"We can't leave now. Here comes Morticia," said Tully.

"Welcome, honored guests," said Morticia. "May I offer you a snack before the séance? Snake innards? Rat whiskers?"

Margaret was about to faint. But a hideous and deafening noise brought her to her senses.

15

5.
Hello, Fester

"**L**et the séance begin!" cried Gomez, as Lurch struck another deafening chord on the organ.

Sitting at a round table, with a crystal ball at the center, were Morticia, Gomez, Granny, Wednesday, Pugsley, Tully, and Margaret.

Morticia held up a statuette.

"Let us gather, in this house of yearning, on this day of heartsick loss, at this table of woe," said Morticia. Then she asked, "Is everyone comfortable?"

Pugsley and Wednesday began to fight.

"Kids! Aren't they adorable?" said Gomez proudly. "And now, Morticia, my sweet, continue."

"Sing, O spirits! Harken, all souls! Every year on this date, we offer a clarion call to Fester Addams. From generation to generation our beacon to the beyond," said Morticia.

She passed the statuette to Wednesday.

"Do you accept the glorious burden, my child?" said Morticia.

"May it weigh me down through all my melancholy years," replied Wednesday.

"Let us all close eyes and join hands," said Morticia.

"Ow!" cried Granny to Margaret a moment later. "You've got quite a grip on you!"

Granny pulled her arm back. But the hand stayed.

"Ooo! My hand, my hand! She's got my hand!" cackled Granny.

"Eeek!" yelled Margaret, who was left holding Thing. She tried to shake Thing off. She tried to run away. But Thing would not let go!

"Stick around," said Tully. "It's all in fun."

He pulled Margaret back into her chair. Thing ran away. Then Granny took Margaret's hand and held it in her own cold, bony one.

"Go on, Wednesday, dear," said Morticia.

"Let us ransom you from the power of the grave. Tonight, O Death, let us be your plague," said Wednesday.

Suddenly, Granny began breathing hard and fast.

"I feel . . . that he . . . is near to us. Fester Addams, gather your strength and knock three times," said Granny.

First there was silence. Then came three knocks at the door.

KNOCK. KNOCK. KNOCK.

"Did you hear that?!" shouted Granny.

"Ask again, Mama. Quickly!" said Morticia.

Over the noise of the organ, Granny called, "Fester Addams, I demand that you knock again!"

KNOCK! KNOCK! KNOCK!

"He's at the door!" shouted Gomez.

Gomez ran to the door and opened it. Before him was the face of his long-lost brother, Fester Addams.

For several moments, Gomez and Fester just stared at each other. The family — and Margaret and Tully — gathered round them.

"Could it be?" said Morticia.

"Is that him?" asked Granny.

"Is it possible?" asked Tully, acting the most surprised of all.

Gomez looked at Morticia. Then he looked at Fester. Then back at Morticia. Then at Fester.

Finally Gomez shouted, "Fester, my brother!"

And Fester answered, "Gomez!"

As they embraced, Abigail, who was dressed for the part she was about to play, quietly slipped in the doorway.

"Gut evenink," she said. "My name is Dr. Pinder-Schloss. I haf come to explain some tinks to you."

6.
Aaahhh!

"Tell us everything!" said Gomez. "We're all ears."

Gomez felt a tap on his shoulder. It was Thing.

"Sorry about that, Thing," said Gomez. "I forgot that some of us are all hand."

"The story is most amazink," said Dr. Pinder-Schloss. "I promise I vill leave notink out."

"Who's she kidding with that phony accent?" whispered Margaret.

"Shhh!" said Tully, poking Margaret in the ribs.

"Ze story begins in Miami, near ze Bermuda Triangle," said Dr. Pinder-Schloss. "Fester vas found zere, tangled in ze tuna net! It vas only last month, during ze Hurricane Helga. Ze sky, it vas black. Ze vaves, zey vere valls of doom. Zey drag him from ze ocean, from ze very mouth of death.

I'm tellink you, it vas too much! Ze Florida Department of ze Fish unt Game do tests unt tests unt more tests. Lo and behold — go tell it on ze mountaintop! — tests show zees man is your bruzzer! Zey gif him to me and after all zees years, I am bringink him home to you!"

"What a story!" cried Gomez. Again he threw his arms around his brother.

"You're back!" said Tully cheerfully. "Back to share your joys, back to share your sorrows, back to share — well, hey — everything!"

"That story was ridiculous," mumbled Margaret.

"Here, show me again how this finger thing works," said Tully, trying to keep Margaret busy.

He handed her the ancient finger trap. In a flash, Margaret's fingers were back inside it.

"Not again!" whispered Margaret, trying to pull free.

"Welcome home, dear Fester," said Morticia.

"I'll be staying for a week at least," said Fester.

"For a week? But where would you go? You're home now," said Gomez.

"I've got to get back to Miami. I've got a lot of things cooking in the Bermuda Triangle," said Fester.

"Nobody goes in and out of the Bermuda Triangle," said Wednesday, suspiciously. "Everyone knows that."

"Oh, my little vun," said Abigail, "zere is so much you do not understandt."

She pinched Wednesday's cheek. Hard. Wednesday did not take her eyes off the man who claimed to be her long-lost uncle Fester.

"Come, Fester, darling," said Morticia. "You must be tired. I'll show you to your room."

On the dresser in his room, Fester found a picture of himself with Gomez when they were boys. Another picture, set in an expensive leather frame, showed the identical faces of two beautiful girls. Written under one was the name *Flora*. Under the other was the name *Fauna*.

"Such sweet memories," mumbled Fester.

"Let me help you unpack," said Morticia.

"No! It's all right!" cried Fester. He tried to grab his bag of burglary equipment. But Morticia got to it first.

"A crowbar . . . dynamite . . . cyanide. Fester, you know we'd never run out of these things," said Morticia, shaking her head. "Well, good night. Sleep tight. If you're good, something creepy will bite!"

"Good night. It's great to be home," said Fester.

When Morticia left, he studied the picture of Flora and Fauna again.

"Now those are faces to dream about," said Fester to himself.

He turned out the lights, sunk down into the

deep, soft mattress, and closed his eyes. He was just drifting off to sleep when he heard the creaking of the door.

"Who . . . who . . . who's there?" called Fester, reaching for his knife.

He felt something creeping, creeping, crawling, crawling up the side of the bed and onto his leg.

Fester's scream shattered the night.

"Aaaahhhh!"

7.
Now You See It . . .

Gomez looked in on Fester early the next morning. He found Thing curled up on his chest like a sleeping cat.

"Thing must have surprised Fester with a welcome-home visit last night. I knew I heard screams of joy," said Gomez to himself.

Gomez gently lifted a sleeping Thing from Fester's chest and slipped him into his jacket pocket.

The movement woke Fester. Clutching his knife, Fester leaped on Gomez.

"Eeya!" shouted Gomez. He flipped Fester and himself backward, then landed on his feet with a smile.

"It's good to have you back, old boy! Let's go get some breakfast," said Gomez.

In the kitchen, the walls dripped with sweat, and smoke crawled along the floorboards.

"Have a seat," said Granny. "You're just in

time." She put a steaming bowl in front of Fester.

"What is this?" asked Fester, staring at the bubbling mess before him.

"It's Mama's specialty," said Morticia. "You should start with the eyes. They're most delicious."

"May I have seconds?" asked Wednesday.

"Me, too!" said Pugsley.

"Here, take mine," said Fester. "I'm not very hungry."

"Let's go then," said Gomez. "To the vault!"

"Sounds good to me!" said Fester, trying not to jump for joy.

Gomez led Fester to his den. He took a book from the shelf. Fester could read the title clearly. The book was called *Greed*. Fester smiled as the secret panel turned.

They found themselves in a chamber on the other side. Hundreds of rusty chains hung down from the ceiling. Gomez pulled one. He and Fester dropped through a trapdoor like two stones down a well. They slid down a long twisting slide and landed by a dirty river.

"Smell that steaming air!" cried Gomez.

Fester could hardly keep from gagging. He tried telling himself it would be over soon. All he had to do was remember the way to the vault. Then he and Abigail would be rich!

Gomez led him into a gondola. They sailed down

the mucky river until they came to a huge door with an equally huge combination lock on it.

"Two to the right, ten to the left, then around to . . . ?" said Gomez.

"Um . . . five?" guessed Fester.

"What? How could you forget? It's eleven! Two, ten, eleven. That's eyes, fingers, and toes," said Gomez.

"Ah, yes, yes. How silly of me," said Fester, licking his lips greedily.

Slowly the door opened. Fester pushed forward to see the vault. But instead of the vault, he found himself in a room stranger than any he had seen before. It was filled with torn-up old furniture, big steel traps, and strange animal trophies.

"Welcome back to our secret spot! *Sanctus sanctorum!*" said Gomez happily.

"It's great to be back," said Fester, playing along as best he could.

"Let's have a drink, old boy," said Gomez. He was struggling to open a well-sealed crate. "I'm busy here. Pick what you like."

Fester reached out and pulled a bottle from the shelf. As soon as he did, the bar spun around once.

That's when Fester saw it. It was only for an instant. But he saw it! And it was amazing!

8.
Forgetful

Fester shuddered with delight. He had seen the vault! It was filled with all the gold, jewels, and priceless treasures he and Abigail had dreamed of.

As quickly as the bar spun him around, it spun him back. Gomez never even noticed that Fester had gone.

"It's showtime!" called Gomez, lifting an armful of old film cans from the open crate. "Get ready for a trip down Memory Lane."

He turned out the lights, and an old screen lit up with pictures. There were Gomez and Fester on vacation. They were scaring little children. They were burying a sunbather in the sand, head and all.

"What fun we had," said Fester.

Then came Gomez and Fester as teenagers, dressed up in tuxedos. Gomez was smoking a cigar.

"Here we are at the debutante ball!" said Gomez. "Do you remember that fateful night?"

"You smoked your first cigar," said Fester.

"What? I started smoking cigars when I was five! You know mother made me," said Gomez.

Fester turned back to the screen. It was filled with the faces he had seen in the picture in his room.

"Flora and Fauna. What a pair!" said Fester, trying to make up for his mistake about the cigar.

"Fester, can you ever forgive me?" asked Gomez.

"For what?" asked Fester.

"For trying to steal Flora and Fauna from you. I never loved them. But I went after them anyway. I was insanely jealous at how much they liked you. I didn't want you to have them," said Gomez. "But I didn't mean to drive you off. Not to the Bermuda Triangle. I swear it!"

"Water under the bridge. Forgiven and forgotten," said Fester.

"Thanks, old boy!" said Gomez. He grabbed Fester and got him in a headlock.

"Say it!" said Gomez, playfully. "Say the password!"

"The password?" gasped Fester. "I . . . I . . . please . . . I'm choking . . . please!"

"You couldn't have forgotten our password," said Gomez, letting Fester go. "We used the word a hundred times a day."

"That was a long time ago. We were kids," said Fester.

Just then, Morticia appeared at the door.

"It's time for the charity auction," she said. "We don't want to be late."

The auction was held at the Bayshore Women's Club. Judge Womack was in charge.

"This rare finger trap was donated by the Addams family," said Judge Womack. "We'll start the bidding at five thousand dollars."

"Bah! Not enough!" said Gomez. "Twenty thousand!"

"Thirty!" called Morticia.

"What are they doing?" whispered Margaret. "They're bidding on something they already own."

"Shhh," said Tully.

"*Cara mia*! You excite me!" cried Gomez. "Forty thousand!"

"Fifty!" said Morticia. "It's for charity, after all."

"My divine one, the trap is yours," said Gomez.

"Sold to Morticia Addams!" called Judge Womack.

Fester got his hands on the finger trap before

anyone else could. He wanted to admire the trea-
sure he hoped would someday be his. Without
thinking, he stuck his fingers inside.

"How do I get this off?" said Fester.

"You must have forgotten," said Morticia, setting Fester free. "There's a trick to it."

Fester walked off, wriggling his fingers.

Morticia and Gomez looked at each other. They
were both wondering the same thing.

9.
He Must Be Upset

"I can't believe it, Thing. Fester didn't know how to take off the finger trap!" shouted Gomez. "That trap was a party favor at his tenth birthday. He wore it for two years straight! Mother had to teach him to eat with his feet!"

Toot! Toot! Whenever Gomez was upset, he played with his train set. *Toot! Toot!*

"All right, my speeding locomotives. Get ready to run for your lives!" said Gomez, setting three trains on a collision course.

Thing jumped back from the track. When Gomez was this upset, watch out!

"What's more," continued Gomez, "he forgot our secret combination. He couldn't remember our password. And he didn't even know that I smoked my first cigar when I was five!"

Thing and Gomez paced back and forth as the trains whizzed around the track on their journey to doom.

Upstairs, Morticia sat with Pugsley and Wednesday.

Toot! Toot! They heard the trains whistling around the track downstairs.

"Uh-oh," said Pugsley. "Father's playing with his trains again."

"He must be upset," said Wednesday.

"Yes, children. Hobbies are a very bad sign," said Morticia.

"I know what he's worried about," said Wednesday. "He doesn't know if that man is really Uncle Fester, does he?"

"It's late now, darlings, and time for bed," said Morticia. "We can talk about this in the morning. Did you brush your teeth and wash behind your ears?"

"I did. I'm sorry," said Pugsley.

Suddenly, the house started to shake.

"The first explosion," said Wednesday.

Wednesday and Pugsley were in bed for the night when Fester decided it was time to get up and get busy.

He strapped on his safecracking tools and took out his explosives. Then he headed for Gomez' den and went straight for the book called *Greed.*

"Vault of riches, here I come!" said Fester as the secret panel turned.

"Oh, no!" he said when he reached the other side. He had forgotten all about the ceiling filled with rusty chains. Now, which was he supposed to pull?

Fester had no idea, so he grabbed the closest one.

"Wait! I'm going the wrong way!" cried Fester. Instead of being dropped straight down like before, Fester was being pulled straight up at lightning speed. Up through space, up through a hole in the ceiling, up through Pugsley's tank of man-eating fish.

Then suddenly, he was falling down, down, down a cold, dark tunnel. He landed outside. Morticia was there waiting for him.

"Sleepless night?" asked Morticia. "Come walk with me."

Fester followed Morticia to the family grave-yard.

"Here lies Aunt LaBorgia — executed by a firing squad," said Morticia. "Here is Cousin Fledge — torn limb from limb by four wild horses. And here is darling Uncle Eimar — buried alive. They were psychopaths and fiends. We must learn from their mistakes."

The graves began to moan in the darkness.

Gulp. Fester swallowed hard.

"Of course you know the family motto," said Morticia. *"We gladly feast on those who would subdue us.* You would not subdue us, would you?"

"Never," said Fester. "I am an Addams."

10.
An Amazink Theory

"**T**hey're on to me, Mother!" whispered Fester into the phone.

"I'll be right over," said Abigail.

Downstairs in the kitchen, Granny was washing the dishes. Lurch was drying. Thing was stacking. And Morticia was drinking a cup of hemlock tea to calm herself down.

"Gomez has been playing with his train set all night. And the children are worried sick. Tell me, what can I do, Mama?" asked Morticia.

Granny wiped her hands and picked up a large, gray, well-used book.

"We'll look under *Husbands*," she said. "Here we are. *Husbands Turned Into Toads or Reptiles*. No. That's not right. *Cranky Husbands*. No. *Anxious, Suspicious Husbands*. That should do it."

"What does it say?" asked Morticia.

Thing turned the page for Granny. Granny began to read aloud.

"Drain all his blood and replace it overnight with vinegar. Leave a headless rooster beneath his pillow. Smear his forehead, palms, and feet with tears from a weeping monkey. Add milk — "

"Oh, Mother! I can't do that! I'm surprised at you," said Morticia. *"Milk!"*

Meanwhile, Fester quietly let Abigail into the house and led her upstairs to his room.

"I haven't been able to get into the vault yet," said Fester. "But they know I'm not who I say I am. I'm sure of it."

"Don't worry. Remember, I am a doctor. Dr. Pinder-Schloss. I vill make everytink all right," said Abigail, slipping into her accent.

Fester brought Abigail down to the drawing room and waited outside.

"It's good you're here tonight," said Morticia. "Gomez is having some doubts about Fester. Do you think he should talk with Fester?"

"Ha!" cried Gomez. He walked to the door and spoke loudly, so Fester could hear. "I would talk with Fester if that *were* Fester. But that's not! That's an imposter. A faker! A phony! A fraud!"

"Calm down, Mr. Addams, I beleef I can help you," said Abigail. "Zere is an amazink theory.

34

Ze theory of displacement. Is zis familiar? Yes? Or no?"

"Well, I must say, it isn't," said Gomez. "Do you know it, Morticia?"

Morticia shook her head.

"Well, it is very, very excitink. I vill explain it to you," said Abigail.

"Is it unpleasant?" asked Gomez hopefully.

"Deeply," answered Abigail.

"Then speak to us!" said Gomez and Morticia together.

"It goes like dis," began Abigail. "Long ago you drive avay your very own bruzzer. Be gone, you say! Go! But zen you feel a monster growing inside you. Who is ze monster? Ze monster is *guilt!*"

"Amazink! I mean, amazing," said Gomez.

"Your bruzzer returns," continued Abigail. "You feel guilty, so vat do you do? You *displace!*"

"I do?" said Gomez.

"He does?" said Morticia.

"Of course! Your brain cells, zey bubble, zey collide! You luff him, but you hate him. Luff, hate, luff, hate. Zis is a very common psychosis. I am seeink it every day," said Abigail.

"So, it's displacement. And here I thought Fester was the problem," said Gomez. "He's certainly moody . . ."

"And secretive . . ." said Morticia.

"And backstabbing!" said Gomez. "Why, he *is* Fester! Thank you, Dr. Pinder-Schloss! Thank you!"

"I do vat I can," said Dr. Pinder-Schloss with a smile.

11.
Toad on a Stick

"Tonight's the night," said Abigail. "The family is going to the children's school play. The house will be empty."

"But I want to go to the play, too," said Fester. "I've been helping Pugsley and Wednesday practice their parts."

"What?!!" said Abigail, shaking Fester till his teeth rattled. "You can't go to the play. We must get into the vault tonight. This is your mother speaking. Do you understand?"

"Y-y-yes, Mother," answered Fester.

"There, there. That's better," said Abigail, patting Fester's bald head.

Fester was feeling a little dizzy, so he went up to the roof for some air. He found Gomez there, looking out at his beloved swamp.

"Fester! I'm so glad to see you, old boy," said Gomez. "What a fool I was to doubt you. Dr.

Pinder-Schloss explained everything to me. You see, I was suffering from displacement. It's a common psychosis. Isn't that grand?"

"Is it?" asked Fester.

"Of course it is! Now, look at our magnificent home. Ooze. Quicksand. Fumes. Toxic waste. It's all ours, old man," said Gomez.

"I don't belong here," said Fester. "You have a beautiful wife. Wonderful kids. I'd just be in the way."

"In the way?" cried Gomez. "Don't ever even think that! We're brothers. You belong here."

That night, Fester sat moping in his room while the rest of the family got ready to go to the play.

On their way out, Wednesday and Pugsley poked their heads into Fester's room.

"Are you sure you can't come?" asked Pugsley.

"You promised you'd help us," said Wednesday.

"Well, I changed my mind. I have other plans!" said Fester, sharply.

The Addams family filed out of their black stretch limousine a short time later. They walked into the school in a line, waving like movie stars to the crowds who had gathered to watch them.

The first people they met inside were Margaret and Tully Alford, with their son, Tully, Jr.

"Isn't he adorable?" said Margaret, showing off Tully, Jr., in his costume. "I made it myself."

"It's charming," said Morticia. "What is he? A lizard?"

"An *elf*. He's an *elf*," said Margaret.

"So, Gomez," said Tully. "Where's Fester this evening?"

"He's being moody, as usual," said Gomez. "We're all out on a jaunt, and he's home alone in that big, empty house."

"What a shame," said Tully, looking very serious. Inside he was jumping for joy. If Fester was home, it could only mean one thing. He would be breaking into the vault that very night.

"Toad on a stick! Get your red-hot toad on a stick!" cried Granny. "How about you, fella? Can't enjoy the show without your toad on a stick."

"I would rather die than eat one of those things," said Judge Womack.

"May I have everyone's attention, please?" said the teacher. "It's time for our show to begin."

Just then, the auditorium door opened and Fester hurried inside. He made his way down the aisle and sat next to Gomez.

"I couldn't let the kids down," whispered Fester.

"Psst," whispered Granny. "I saved you one."

And she passed Fester a red-hot toad on a stick.

12.
One Big, Happy Family

"Thank you for coming to the play tonight," said Wednesday.

"Nothing could have kept me away," said Fester, tucking her into bed. "You were really terrific. Especially when you cut off Pugsley's arm."

" 'O, from this time forth, my thoughts be bloody or nothing worth,' " recited Wednesday.

"Bravo!" said Fester. "And now, it's time to go to sleep."

Wednesday held out her headless doll. Fester kissed its empty neck. Next she held out the severed head. Fester kissed that, too. Then he turned out the light.

Neither of them heard the muffled screams outside the window.

"*Mrrrpf, mrrrpf!*" cried Abigail. She was wrapped up in a thorny vine like a mummy.

Earlier that night, she had gone back to the Addamses' house to look for Fester. The door was locked and no one was home. When she tried to climb in a window, she stepped on the vine.

"I never should have used him. He's not to be trusted," she said as the vine began wrapping itself around her ankles and up her body.

Abigail stayed wrapped up till morning when Lurch found her.

"Arrrrowwl," he growled as he chopped the vines from her body with a rusty axe.

Abigail staggered into the kitchen, picking vines from her teeth and hair.

"Doctor! You were so right!" said Gomez, seeing nothing unusual about her behavior. "Fester fit right in last night. The displacement is over!"

"Vell, isn't dat nice," said Abigail, glaring at Fester as she spit out another thorn.

"Does he really have to go back to the Bermuda Triangle with you?" asked Wednesday.

"We want him to stay here," said Pugsley.

"He must come vith me, children," said Abigail.

"We've planned a farewell party for you, Fester," said Morticia. "We've invited the whole Addams clan."

Fester was truly touched at the thought. He looked gratefully at Morticia and Gomez, hoping Abigail wouldn't see. But she did.

"Fester, vill you valk me out?" Abigail said.

As soon as they were outside, she shouted, "What do you think you're doing?"

"It's all right, Mother. I'm completely in control," said Fester.

"They are *not* your family, Gordon. I am. Remember that," hissed Abigail.

"Yes, Mother," said Fester.

That night, Morticia, Gomez, Granny, Lurch, Pugsley, Wednesday, and Fester walked into the ballroom together. Each of them carried a flickering black candle.

Fester could hardly believe his eyes. The black marble floor glistened. Black drapes fluttered in the breeze at open windows. The food bubbled and moaned. It was awful and beautiful at the same time.

"For me?" said Fester.

"All for you," said Morticia.

Lurch began to play the organ.

"*Cara mia*, how long has it been since we've waltzed?" asked Gomez, taking Morticia in his arms.

"Hours, darling, hours!" said Morticia.

"Wednesday, may I have this dance?" said Fester.

"Delighted, to be sure," said Wednesday.

Pugsley danced with Granny while Thing joined Lurch for a duet on the organ. They were one big, happy family.

For the moment, anyway.

13.
Ooot, Ooot, Ooot

The guests began to arrive around eight.

Slosh Addams, who looked more like a toad than a man, came with his wife, Lois.

Digit Addams had all four arms around his date's shoulders.

Lumpy Addams wore a suit so loud you needed earplugs to look at it.

Dexter and Donald Addams, Gomez's two-headed cousin, nodded to each other and began to speak.

"I wonder . . . I wonder . . . what happened . . . what happened . . . to Fester . . . to Fester," they said.

"He's here. But I guess he's fixing his hair," said Gomez, with a wink. Behind him, he heard a familiar voice.

"Well, speaking of hair!" cried Gomez.

Cousin It walked in the door. He was all hair from the top of his head down to his shoes. You couldn't see what he was wearing, except for the black homburg hat on top of his head.

"*Bleep gibber, ooot, ooot,*" said Cousin It.

"You're absolutely right, old man!" said Gomez. "It's been far too long since we've seen each other."

Cousin It looked around the room. He was studying the women. When he came to Margaret Tully, he looked no further. He ran his fingers through his hair, then patted it into place.

"*Ooot gibber, bleep,*" he said to Gomez.

"Of course, you're excused," said Gomez. "I'll catch you later."

Margaret was on the dance floor with Tully. She was hanging onto him for dear life.

"Don't let me out of your sight for a minute!" she was saying. Then she felt the tap on her shoulder.

"*Oot, oot, oot,*" said Cousin It. Before Margaret knew what was happening, Cousin It took her in his arms and whirled her across the room.

It was getting late and Fester still had not shown up. Morticia was beginning to worry.

"Wednesday, could you run upstairs and check on your uncle?" she asked.

"Yes, Mother," said Wednesday. She hurried up to Fester's room.

There was no answer when she knocked on the door, so Wednesday went inside. She heard the water running in the bathroom. When it went off, she could hear voices.

"I'm counting on you, Gordon," said Abigail. "Don't let me down."

"I'll do my best, Mother. But it's not going to be easy. There are people everywhere," said Fester.

"Just do it and stop whining," said Abigail.

"All right. I'll try my best to reach the vault tonight. But if I can't, then that's it, okay, Mother?" said Fester, trying his best not to whine.

Wednesday's face turned red. Her body grew stiff. She was furious.

"You are a fake! I knew it!" she cried.

Abigail and Fester spun around. The razor Abigail was using to shave Fester's head gleamed in the light.

"Come here, little vun. Ve von't hurt you," said Abigail.

Fester froze. He didn't know what to do. He didn't want Wednesday to get hurt. But he was afraid to go against his mother's wishes.

"Get her, you fool!" yelled Abigail. She pushed Fester toward Wednesday.

Wednesday ran as fast as she could back to her room. She slammed the door behind her.

Fester was still under his mother's power. He ran after Wednesday and kicked open the door just in time to see her disappearing through a trapdoor in her floor. Once it closed, Fester could not open it again.

Wednesday slid down a ramp. She landed outside near the vines that had grabbed Abigail. She stood up, dusted herself off, then disappeared into the night.

14.
Shall We Dance?

"**A**rrrowwl!" growled Lurch, announcing the arrival of Flora and Fauna Amor.

Twenty-five years had passed since the picture in Fester's room had been taken. But Flora and Fauna were still as beautiful — and as crazy — as ever.

Looking at their picture, one would have thought they were twins. But they were more. Flora and Fauna were Siamese twins, joined at the waist.

"I cannot see! I'm blinded by beauty!" cried Gomez.

"You're such a flirt," said Flora.

"You always flirted with me. Remember?" said Fauna.

"No, he flirted with *me*!" said Flora.

"Hello," said Morticia. "I'm so glad you could come. I've heard so much about you."

"Oh, Morticia, I just hate you for nabbing this darling man!" said Flora.

"He was mine," said Fauna.

"No, he was *mine*," said Flora.

"Flora, Fauna, how can I compete. You're twice the woman I am," said Morticia.

Just then Tully, who was searching for Margaret, passed by.

"Tully, meet the Amor twins. They're waiting for Fester. Amuse them while I go look for him," said Gomez.

"I saw him first," said Flora, batting her eyelashes in Tully's direction.

"Ignore her," said Fauna, running a long, red fingernail down Tully's cheek.

The next thing Tully knew, four arms were dragging him onto the dance floor. It was a little awkward at first, but soon Tully got the hang of dancing with Flora and Fauna. In fact, the three of them — or was it two of them? — were quite graceful.

"We were so surprised when Gomez called to tell us Fester was back," said Flora.

"He and Gomez seem to be getting along very well — considering," said Fauna.

"Considering what?" asked Tully.

"Considering the fact that Fester is the king of the castle now that he's back," said Flora.

"That's right," said Fauna. "He's the older brother, so he gets it all. The house, the money — you name it."

"Oh, really?" said Tully. "I didn't know that."

"Fester is still single, isn't he?" asked Flora.

"Why, yes, I suppose he is," said Tully, who was only half listening now.

"You're cute, too," said Fauna.

"Thanks," said Tully. "I'm flattered. But I've got to go."

Tully blew them each a kiss and ran off the dance floor. He ran right past Margaret, who was dancing cheek to cheek with Cousin It.

"Glibber gleep, gleep," said It.

"Oh, you're just too much!" giggled Margaret.

Tully had no time to worry about Margaret. There was someone important he had to see. He slipped out of the ballroom and headed for the front door. Abigail stopped him.

"We're in trouble," she said. "That little cockroach, Wednesday, knows everything!"

"Not to worry," said Tully. "I've got Plan B."

"What is it?" asked Abigail.

"I'll explain later," said Tully, heading out the door.

A moment later, the bell rang at Judge Womack's house. Judge Womack opened the door, ready to blast any fool who had the nerve to bother him.

Tully didn't bother waiting for a greeting.

"How would you like to be rid of the Addams family — for good?" he asked.

A huge grin spread across Judge Womack's face.

"Those words are music to my ears," he said. "Won't you come in?"

15.
Keep Out!

Fester climbed back through the window of his room.

"I can't find Wednesday anywhere. She's disappeared," he said.

"It doesn't matter now. Just pull yourself together and get to the party. Otherwise they'll get suspicious," said Abigail.

Morticia grabbed Fester as he walked into the ballroom.

"Everyone! Your attention, please," said Morticia. "Fester, our treasured guest of honor, has arrived."

Before Fester knew what was happening, Morticia grabbed his arm and spun him across the room. He went whirling like a top and landed face-to-face with Gomez. Gomez was dressed like a warrior, with five shining swords.

"It's time to dance the mamushka!" cried

Gomez. Morticia, Granny, and all the other Addams women picked up tambourines and began rapping out a warrior's beat. Slowly, Gomez began to circle around Fester.

Beads of sweat dripped down Fester's forehead as Gomez began throwing the swords in his direction. Somehow, Fester managed to catch them and throw them back.

"The Addamses have been doing the mamushka since the beginning of time," said Gomez. "The tradition continues!"

Gomez threw the swords faster and faster. Fester caught them and threw them back. The two brothers were dancing all the while.

"Fester, you amaze me!" said Gomez, proudly. "You haven't missed a . . ."

Just then, Fester missed his first step. When he looked up, all five swords were coming at him at once. He caught the first! The second! The third! The fourth! He had two swords in each hand. He couldn't hold another. The fifth was on its way. It was coming toward him. Fester opened his mouth to scream. . . .

The sword dropped down his throat. Fester quickly pulled it out, and the crowd went wild, singing and cheering. Fester was actually starting to enjoy himself.

How did I do that? he wondered.

Flora and Fauna were the most impressed of all.

"Why, Fester, that was remarkable," said Fauna.

"You're as brave and dashing as ever," said Flora.

"Thank you, ladies," said Fester. He danced a few more steps of the mamushka, just to show off.

When the party was over, Fester danced all the way up to his room.

"What's the matter with you?" snapped Abigail. "I tell you over and over, that is *not* your family. *I* am your family. So calm down."

"Sorry, Mother," said Fester, coming to his senses.

After all the guests were gone, Morticia realized that she had not seen Wednesday since she had sent her to look for Fester. She looked all over the house.

"Where could she be, Gomez?" said Morticia.

"Don't fret, my darling. We'll find her," said Gomez.

He ran upstairs and got an ancient map of the grounds.

"We'll spread out," said Gomez. "Morticia, you search the swamp. Pugsley, check the bottomless pit. Lurch, take the abandoned well. I'll take the abyss. Granny, you take the ravine."

Thing came running up to lend a hand.

"That's the spirit, Thing. Come with me!" said Gomez.

The search went on for hours. Finally just outside Gate, as dawn was beginning to break, Gomez saw a dark shape covering Great-great-grandfather Addams' tomb. It was Wednesday. She was fast asleep.

"My sweet one!" whispered Gomez, not wanting to wake her.

He picked her up quietly and was about to walk through Gate. But Gate could not open. It rattled miserably on its hinges. It was locked tight with heavy chains and police tape. There were signs posted all over. NO TRESPASSING! COURT ORDER! ADDAMS FAMILY — KEEP OUT!

"What is going on?" cried Gomez.

16.
Big Trouble

"**L**et me in that house!" said Granny. "I'll get my book of spells and fix whoever did this!"

"Don't take another step!" called Tully, running down the walk, waving a piece of paper. "I have a legal document here. It says you have to be at least one thousand yards from that house."

"But it's *my* house!" cried Gomez.

"Not anymore. It belongs to the oldest living Addams descendant. That would be one Fester Addams," said Tully.

"Fester adores Gomez. He wouldn't do something like this," said Morticia.

"It just so happens that Fester is afraid of Gomez. Seeing the twins, Flora and Fauna, brought back all the bitter memories of when they were rivals," said Tully.

"Those twins meant nothing to me! Fester knows that," said Gomez. "Let me see Fester. I want to talk to him."

"Sorry. No can do," said Tully. "Fester is feeling very hurt right now. The best thing to do is leave him alone. Better yet, just leave."

"But that man isn't even Uncle Fester," said Wednesday, rubbing her eyes. All the shouting had awakened her.

"Justice shall prevail!" cried Gomez. "I will take this to court. Let the courts decide!"

The following afternoon, the Addams family went before a judge. Unfortunately it was Judge Womack, the Addamses' unhappy next-door neighbor.

"Given the facts as they have been presented to me," said Judge Womack, tossing the golf ball that broke his window up in the air, "I find in favor of Fester Addams. By the power vested in me, I declare him rightful owner of the Addams estate and all properties and possessions contained therein."

With a whack of the gavel, the Addamses' day in court was done.

The family went back to the mansion to pack

up the few things they were allowed to take with them. Gomez took the golf ball that Judge Womack returned to him after the trial. Morticia took Cleo, her flesh-eating plant. Granny had her big, black cauldron. Wednesday had her headless doll. Pugsley had his chemistry set. Lurch had his favorite tree. And Thing dragged along a little red wagon filled with his rings and his glove.

Not a word was spoken as the family piled into the car and drove off to the seedy Wampum Court Bungalows.

They tried their best to make their bungalow cozy.

"Arrrowwl," growled Lurch as he ripped up chunks of asphalt and planted his tree.

"That's very nice, Lurch," said Morticia.

Morticia hung up a painting she had brought along from the mansion.

"I like it," said Granny, patting Morticia's hand.

"The family is together. That's the important thing. Isn't that right, Gomez?" said Morticia.

"Huh?" said Gomez, looking at Morticia as though he had never seen her before. Poor Gomez. He was slumped down in a musty old chair. He had no energy. He had no hope.

Wednesday lovingly put her arms around her father.

"Would you like a cigar?" she asked.

"They're very bad for you," said Gomez flatly.

"But, Father . . ." said Wednesday. She was starting to worry.

"This place isn't so bad," said Pugsley. "They even put candy in the bathroom."

"That's a bar of soap you are nibbling on, dear," said Morticia.

"I'll have one of those," said Gomez.

He unwrapped the bar of soap and started chewing it slowly. Wednesday and Morticia looked at each other with fear in their eyes.

The Addams family was in big trouble.

17.
Action!

"We are Addamses, and we will not submit!" said Morticia, rallying the family. "Poison us, strangle us, break our bones. We will come back for more. And why?"

"Because we like it!" said Granny.

"Because we're Addamses!" said Pugsley.

"Because . . . we're . . . *burp*!" said Gomez. Soap bubbles floated from his mouth up to the ceiling.

The family, except for Gomez, who couldn't rally if he tried, leaped to action.

Wednesday and Pugsley set up a refreshment stand. They sold poisons of every kind.

"Five cents a cup! Come and get it!" called Wednesday.

Lurch passed by. He was going to sell vacuum cleaners door-to-door.

"Have a cup," said Pugsley. "It's on the house."

Lurch drank it in one gulp.

"Arrrowwl," he growled. Flames shot out of his mouth as he set off down the road.

A Girl Scout selling cookies came next.

"Is this made from *real* lemons? I only like all-natural foods, you know," she said.

"It's natural," said Pugsley.

"I'll tell you what," said the Girl Scout. "I'll buy a cup from you if you'll buy a box of Girl Scout cookies from me."

"Are they made from *real* Girl Scouts?" asked Wednesday.

Meanwhile, Morticia landed a job teaching at a day-care center. A group of ten toddlers was gathered around her for story time.

". . . and so the witch lured Hansel and Gretel into the candy house, by promising them more sweets. She told them to look in the oven. She was about to push them in, when, lo and behold, Hansel pushed the poor defenseless witch into the oven instead. The witch was burned alive and died a horrible, painful death. Now, boys and girls, what do you think that feels like?"

The toddlers wailed and cried for the rest of the day.

Back at the bungalow, Morticia found Gomez in the same place she had left him. He was eating junk food and watching TV.

"He's been doing it all day," said Wednesday.

"Dinner is going to be a little late," said Granny. "I'm going to go catch it now."

She left the bungalow calling, "Here, kitty, kitty, kitty . . ."

That night before going to sleep, Wednesday asked Morticia, "Mother, if that man isn't Uncle Fester, then who is he?"

"I don't know, darling. I wish I did," answered Morticia.

"And why is that lady doctor doing all this?" asked Wednesday.

"It's hard to say. Sometimes people have had terrible childhoods. And sometimes they just haven't found their special place in life. And sometimes they're just mad dogs from the darkest depths, who must be destroyed," said Morticia.

"Good night, Mother," said Wednesday.

"Good night, my sweet," said Morticia.

As soon as everyone had fallen asleep, Morticia slipped out the door and headed for the mansion.

18.
Oooh! The Rack!

"**W**e've been expecting you," said Tully. There was a mean glint in his eye as he opened the door.

"I would like to speak with Fester," said Morticia, stepping inside.

Thing, who had secretly followed Morticia to the mansion, made a mad dash for the road. He had to get help. Fast!

He stuck out his thumb and tried to hitch a ride back to the motel. For some reason he could not understand, no one would stop for him. So he grabbed the bumper of the next car that passed and held on for dear life.

Inside the mansion, Morticia was being tied to the torture rack by Tully and Fester. She could see from the look on Fester's face that he felt torn and upset by what he was doing.

Abigail was in charge of the operation.

"You are a desperate woman, Abigail. You are consumed by greed and bitterness," said Morticia. "We could have been such good friends."

"I don't think so," said Abigail. "Let's talk about the vault."

Morticia had nothing to say on the subject. She was relaxing on the rack.

"Let's get started," said Abigail.

"But, Mother . . ." said Fester.

"Stop whining, Fester. Tully, take over," said Abigail. "Tighten the rack as far as it will go."

"I'd love to, Abigail, but I've got this stomach problem," said Tully. "It happens when I torture people. It's one of those things, you know."

"Do it!" said Abigail.

"Um, Morticia, where's your bathroom, please?" whimpered Tully.

"NOW!!!" shouted Abigail.

Tully swallowed hard and began turning the screws. He heard Morticia's bones creak and then *pop!* It was a horrible sound.

"Oooh," moaned Morticia, enjoying herself.

"Tighter!" said Abigail.

Tully turned the screws again.

"Oh, you're good at this," said Morticia, smiling sweetly in Tully's direction.

While Morticia was being stretched, Thing was racing up to the bungalow for help.

Knock! Knock!

"Who is it? We're paid through Thursday!" called Gomez.

Knock! Knock! Knock!

Gomez opened the door. Thing rushed in and began speaking in sign language.

"Slow down, Thing! I can't follow you when you stutter that way," said Gomez.

Thing decided to try something else. He grabbed a spoon and began tapping out his message in Morse code. He hoped the noise wouldn't wake the rest of the family.

Gomez listened carefully

"Morticia in danger . . . stop! Send help at once . . . stop!" said Gomez. "Good work, Thing. Let's go!"

19.
Hurricane Irene

"Stop! Not the red-hot poker!" cried Fester.

"Is this going to smell bad?" asked Tully.

"Morticia, tell Mother what she wants," begged Fester.

"Tell me, Fester. Which is the real you — the creepy, underhanded monster you've become? Or the creepy, underhanded monster we came to love?" asked Morticia.

"Don't ask me! Please! I don't know!" cried Fester.

"Here, Gordon, dear," said Abigail. "Be my guest."

She handed Fester a red-hot poker from the fire.

Outside, Gate opened without a sound as Gomez and Thing headed for the house.

They looked in the window just in time. Fester

was holding the red-hot poker in his shaking hands. He was inching his way toward Morticia.

"Eeya!" cried Gomez as he came crashing through the window into the den. He did a double back flip and landed by Morticia's side.

"*Cara mia!*" he cried.

"*Mon cher!*" answered Morticia.

"Addams!" shouted Abigail.

Gomez grabbed a sword from the wall. Tully found another.

"Darling, take care!" said Morticia.

Gomez felt Tully coming at him from behind.

"Dirty pool, old man," said Gomez, spinning around.

"This duel is for keeps, Gomez!" said Tully.

Clink! Clink!

With one swift move, Gomez knocked Tully's sword from his hand and flipped Tully over. Tully landed on his knees.

"Gomez, it's me! Your one and only lawyer!" cried Tully.

"Let him up," said Abigail. "Or say good-bye to your dear Morticia."

Gomez turned to find Abigail holding a pistol. It was aimed right at Morticia's head.

"To the vault, Gomez! Move it!" said Abigail.

"Mother, wait . . ." said Fester.

"Stop being such a sniveling baby, Gordon. I

should have left you where I found you," said Abigail.

"All right, all right, I'm going!" said Fester.

He went to the bookcase with Gomez. Gomez reached up to get a book from the shelf.

"No tricks, Gomez," said Fester, loudly enough for Abigail to hear. "That's the wrong book!"

Gomez was reaching for the right book, *Greed*. But Fester stopped him.

"Allow me," Fester said.

Gomez looked into Fester's eyes and understood what Fester was about to do.

Fester pulled a book off the shelf. It was called *Hurricane Irene: Nightmare From Above*.

He turned and showed the cover to Tully and Abigail.

"Put that book down, Gordon!" Tully shrieked. "You don't know what it can do."

"Drop the gun," said Fester.

Abigail did as she was told. She knew that nothing in the Addamses' house was as ordinary as it seemed.

"Keep the book closed. Listen to your mother," she said.

"Never!" answered Fester. "I'll never listen to you again. You never loved me!"

"Come, my love," said Gomez, pulling Morticia to safety.

"But what about Fester?" asked Morticia.

"Behave yourself, Gordon!" said Abigail.

"You're a terrible mother! There! I've said it!" cried Fester.

Then he opened the book. Hurricane Irene rushed out from the covers. The winds blasted Abigail and Tully right out the window.

"This way out, old man!" Gomez called to Fester over the storm.

Fester was trying with all his might to close the book. But the storm was raging out of control. Suddenly, a huge bolt of lightning zapped him!

Fester went crashing to the floor.

20.
No Place Like Home

*B*ong. *Bong. Bong. Bong. Bong. Bong. Bong.* The clock struck seven on Halloween night. It was the Addams family's favorite holiday.

There were jack-o'-lanterns on the stairs. Skeletons in top hats with ropes around their necks hung from the chandeliers. There were black and orange balloons everywhere. A banner with *Happy Halloween* written in blood was tacked to the wall.

Pugsley came downstairs dressed as Uncle Fester. He was wearing a great big coat and his head was bald.

"Look at you!" said Morticia happily.

"Do you like the way I look, Uncle Fester?" asked Pugsley.

"You look great!" said Fester, hugging him. "I'm so glad I can share this night with my family.

My *real* family. Now that I know who I am."

"Oh, to think of that unfortunate woman, Abigail," said Morticia. "Trying to trick you into believing that you were someone named Gordon and that she was your mother."

"You were lost to us for a while there, old boy," said Gomez. "Twenty-five years ago, she really did find you tangled in that tuna net."

"In the Bermuda Triangle!" said Wednesday.

"With no memory," said Pugsley.

"Thank heaven that bolt of lightning zapped you," said Granny. "Best way to bring a memory back."

Ding dong!

"Arrrowwl," growled Lurch, opening the door.

It was Margaret and Cousin It. They were holding hands. They were obviously in love.

Margaret was dressed for Halloween as a fairy princess. Cousin It was dressed as a cowboy. He had a ten-gallon hat on his head and a holster at his waist.

"Trick or treat!" said Margaret. She smiled as she walked past Lurch.

"*Ooot oot glibber,*" said Cousin It.

"Now that everyone's here, let's take a picture," suggested Morticia. "Lurch, will you do the honors?"

"Wednesday, honey, why aren't you wearing a costume?" asked Margaret.

"This *is* my costume," said Wednesday, pointing to her regular clothes. "I'm a homicidal maniac. They look just like everyone else."

"I'll be right back!" called Pugsley. He ran out of the room. When he came back, he had a light bulb in his hand.

"Will you do it, Uncle Fester? For the picture?" asked Pugsley.

"No problem," said Fester. He popped the light bulb into his mouth, and it lit up the room.

"Smile, everyone," said Morticia.

"Arrrowwl," growled Lurch as he snapped a picture of the Addams family on Halloween night.

"All right, everyone, it's time for a game!" said Gomez. "What will it be?"

"Charades?" suggested Margaret.

"*Ooot glibber glip*," said Cousin It.

"Good idea," said Fester. "*Wake the Dead* was my favorite game. We played when we were kids."

"Come on! Everyone out to the graveyard!" said Gomez.

On the way, they passed Abigail and Tully. They were in a glass case, perfectly stuffed and mounted.

Gomez and Morticia were the last to leave.

"Oh, Tish, what a night," sighed Gomez. "Everyone is together at last. What more could we ask for?"

Morticia showed Gomez the baby clothes she was knitting. The little pajamas had three legs.

"Is it true? Are we really going to have another child?" Gomez asked happily.

Morticia nodded. "Yes, *mon cher*."

"*Cara mia!*" cried Gomez, throwing his arms around Morticia.

Then together, they slipped out into the magnificently creepy night to join the rest of the family.